a journey
of
transformation

From the
Heart of
Afghanistan

Mohammad Ali

ILLUMIFY
MEDIA.COM

Published by
Illumify Media Global
www.IllumifyMedia.com
"Write. Publish. Market. *SELL*!"

Paperback ISBN: 978-1-955043-59-5

Cover design by Debbie Lewis

Printed in the United States of America

ONE

Afghanistan the Beautiful

LIFE WAS BEAUTIFUL IN MAZAR-E-SHARIF, Afghanistan, being a kid and enjoying my childhood. I was in second grade at the time and was so excited to go to a parade. I dressed up nicely and went with my school to a parade in the city. As we were walking in this parade, suddenly the Mujahudeen (the religious soldier) fired rockets from the mountains, and everyone started running away. People were crying, and the teachers were trying to hide their children behind walls to keep them safe. I was frantically trying to find my classmates so we could head back home.

This was my first memory of a joyous occasion that turned into chaos in a matter of minutes. After a few months of violent attacks, the Mujahudeen came and took over our city, Mazar-E-Sharif. Dr. Najibullah's government fell apart, and the Mujahudeen took control and turned over our schools to the police stations. I remember them stopping cars on the street, beating and bullying everyone. Order quickly became chaos. Fearful for their safety, many teachers stopped coming to school. Students, too, missed classes because they were scared of the Mujahudeen.

Despite all this, I still enjoyed living among the farms on the hillsides, lush with fruits and vegetables. We had a beautiful home away from the main city of Mazar-E-Sharif. I could not imagine how in once–peaceful Afghanistan a simple town with mud houses and cows and other animals roaming freely would one day turn into a village of terror. Memories are still fresh of chasing kites in the skies, running through the wheat farms, searching for the fallen kites from the kite runners. At this time, and I was the fastest runner of all my friends. Life indeed was beautiful. Every evening I would run to the melon farms and bring a few freshly cut melons up to our roof, inviting my friends to join. We would tell stories, memorize poetry, and challenge each other with mind riddles. I will never forget the smell of fresh naan my mom used to bake on the cylindrical clay oven served with milk and sugar. These things brought feelings of comfort and peace, and they reassured my mind.

But day by day things slowly started to get worse, because the Mujahudeen warlords started to fight with each other. It was very unsafe for me, traveling back and forth to school, because the Mujahudeen would stop me and question what I was doing and why I had schoolbooks. As a young boy, my heart shook with fear every time I would go back and forth to classes. When I got to third grade, one of my older brothers, who was working at the family electronics store, told me I was not learning—even though I was attending school. In his opinion, school was worthless for me. So, he pulled me out and had me start working at the family store with him.

I had to ride on the same bicycle with my brother to work, which took twenty to thirty minutes, and it was very uncomfortable. Slowly, as I learned the electronics business, my brother eventually left me alone with the business while he traveled to different cities to purchase supplies. During this time, I was around ten or eleven years old and had saved some money to purchase my own bicycle. I felt proud of my independence and how smart I was. I also liked a girl in my neighborhood, and we would sometimes hang out at her family's home and talk. I had many dreams about my future, and I would fantasize about what it would look like when I got older. Little did I know that my life would soon turn in a very different direction.

TWO

Becoming a Casualty

ONE AFTERNOON I was passing the police station located near our home, and there were a few young men there that I knew. One of them asked me to come sit with them. I declined and said I wanted to go to the garden near my house. He kept demanding that I come and sit with them for a short visit. Now, this particular police station had recruited some young men to guard their station, and the police provided them with guns. After a few minutes of being with them, one of the young guys pulled out his gun. I warned him that he should not be playing with the gun because someone could get shot. I did not know that that person would be *me*. He turned the AK-47 right toward my chest, so I pushed the gun down toward the ground. After a few seconds, I heard a loud bang and quickly realized that a bullet had hit my left leg right at the knee. The sound was terrifying, and for a few seconds I could not hear, I could not see clearly, and my heart felt faint. It seemed like I had jumped a foot high and then fell to the ground. That's when I saw all the blood. Fear and terror filled my mind. As I lay on the ground bleeding, I heard these young men crying and calling for help because they knew I had been badly hurt.

At that moment, I could not imagine thinking about living or dying or what would happen next in my life. In our village, there were no clinics or hospitals, and no one owned a car. One of the neighbors, an elderly man, came by to help, but he could not do anything medically for me in any way. What he did do, however, was to wait with us and try to flag down any vehicle going by so that I could be taken to the hospital in the main city. Luckily, a military car came along, and the elderly man stopped it and asked the people in it to take me to the hospital. I do not remember how long we had been waiting, but I was going in and out of consciousness because of losing so much blood. I do remember the ride in the military car, though—the bumps over the dirt road and finally arriving at the hospital. After that, I do not remember anything until a few days later when I awoke in the hospital.

THREE

Life Without a Leg

WHEN I AWOKE, I did not know what was going on, but I knew that my arms and legs were tied to the bed. I asked my cousin, who was taking care of me as a nurse, to free my arms and legs. She replied that she could not do so because the doctor had said it was necessary to reduce the risk of losing more blood. I felt as though my legs were numb and that one of my feet was heavy and touching the floor, even though I was still on the hospital bed. I asked my cousin why my feet were on the floor. She gave me the same answer as before—to reduce the risk of bleeding. I continued to go in and out of consciousness for the next couple of days.

The next time I woke up, a policeman was standing over my bed. I heard him say, "Son, do not worry about your leg —a prosthetic leg could be even better than a real leg."

This was the moment I realized I had lost my left leg, and it was so painful and difficult to accept this. My mother was in the room after the policeman left, and I asked her why she allowed the doctor to cut off my leg. I saw the tears rolling down from Mom's eyes and saw that she did not know what to say.

Then she answered, "You would have died if they had not taken off your leg, because you had lost so much blood."

I started to cry. I did not like her answer. This was just not acceptable to me. I looked at her through tears and said, "I would rather die than live with only one leg."

I could not control my emotions; I was crying and saying out loud, "How could I live without a leg? I will not be able to run with my friends or ride my bicycle or do anything on my own."

My cousin overheard me and asked why I was crying. Instead of empathizing with me, she quickly tried to toughen me up by saying, "You are a man. You should not cry." This was her way of comforting me and shutting down my emotions. "If you cry, your mom will be very sad."

The doctor discharged me from the hospital a few days later, and my mom took me back home. Most nights I could not sleep because of the physical pain and mental trauma I suffered. The traumatic memory of that day would continually play over and over again in my mind. Fear and hopelessness were always with me, whether awake or asleep. During the night I would dream that I had both legs and would be running and playing with my friends. Even when I would wake up, I would still think I had my left leg, and would try to walk but would fall to the ground. Every time I would fall, a painful darkness would cover my whole body, as if something were trying to rip my heart from my chest. All of this led me to think my life was worthless and there was nothing good for which to live.

I was looking for possibilities to end my life and be free from the misery I was living with. These thoughts tormented me even more than the physical and emotional pain I was feeling because I saw no way out of my situation. Due to these controlling thoughts, I became more isolated from friends and family. I didn't know how to deal with these thoughts and feelings, and I didn't have anyone to talk me through this psychologically. Where I lived there were no psychologists, therapists, or counselors.

FOUR

Drugs, Depression, and Despair

SOMETIME LATER, I was outside my house and saw a couple of men from my neighborhood sitting under a tree. They were smoking marijuana. We greeted each other, and I sat down next to them. One of them offered me some marijuana and I accepted. After first using it, I wasn't myself for a while. And the dark feelings I had had before came back even worse. At home my parents noticed I was becoming increasingly depressed. They did not know how to respond to my situation or how to treat me or understand my pain. I was convinced they could not care for me emotionally. This continued for a while, and I pondered what I should do.

In 1997, six months after I lost my leg, the Taliban took over the city we lived in—Mazar-E-Sharif, Afghanistan. The Taliban are Sunni Muslim (students of religion). I was about twelve years old at the time. The Taliban killed so many people that I remember walking through the streets and seeing dead bodies all around our village. Mazar-E-Sharif was made up mostly of Hazara, one of the largest ethnic groups in Afghanistan. The Hazaras were mostly

Shiite Muslims (which I was at the time), and this is who the Taliban were targeting.

My older brothers ran away to the mountains just south of the city. My dad took all the remaining family to a city where he knew people from different tribes that were not targeted by the Taliban. He knocked on the doors of everyone he knew and asked secretly if they could shelter us from the Taliban. He was turned down by each one because they feared the Taliban and did not want to take this risk because we were Hazara. Eventually, he located one of his friends who was Hazara and lived in the city, but his family had run to the mountains. Thus, their house was empty. We all stayed there, along with three other Hazara families who had run away from their villages.

FIVE

Dealing with the Enemy

MY FATHER, feeling ever threatened by the Taliban, left the house where we were staying and hid himself in the outskirts of the city. He was constantly on the move to avoid being caught. After a few days, all the food and money we had were gone. I was now the oldest male left behind and became responsible to care for the rest of the family. I ended up going back to our family store and reopening it in order to make money and provide food for our family. The family now included my older brother's wife and their kids plus a few of my younger brothers and sisters.

My mom and some of the other women would travel back to our village often and collect dishes, clothes, and other necessities, but the village was still unlivable. One of the times they went, my mom, my cousin the nurse, another woman, and a few kids were captured by some Taliban and detained in an empty house. The Taliban asked the women to remove their burqas so their faces could be seen. My cousin, one of the youngest and prettiest of the women, was taken to another room and gang raped.

When the group came back from the village to our temporary home, my cousin attempted suicide by taking some pills. When I got home from the family store that day, one of the young boys told me what the Taliban fighters did to my cousin. It so filled my heart with anger that it took my breath away and brought me to tears. I asked my mom if this was true or not, and she said it was. She was in tears herself as she told me they could not do anything to stop it. From that time on, I told my mom that none of the women should travel to the village anymore. It just was not safe.

I personally experienced this cruelty from the Taliban on a daily basis while traveling back and forth to the family store. From that time on, I would travel with other kids to our village. Every street we turned on we came across dead bodies. We even had to watch our steps to avoid the corpses. One time traveling in the village, the Taliban spotted me and approached me.

They slapped my face and kicked me and said, "Tell us the truth: you fought against us, that is why you lost your leg."

Then they put a bullet in their gun and pushed me right to the edge of a big hole and said, "We're going to shoot you in the chest, unless you tell us the truth."

I said, "Okay, just shoot me. I really do not care if I live or die. The truth is I have never touched a gun."

This moment was the opportunity for the Taliban to end my life. I did not have a desire to live anyway, so this threat did not scare me. They removed the gun from my chest and just walked away. I thought to myself, *What has this world given me except pain?* During these dark times, I was collapsing under the fear, uncertainty, anger, anxiety, and torture by the Taliban daily. I could not express these things to my family and cause them even more pain than they had already suffered. I was also the only one who could provide my family with food—there was no one else. After a couple months, the men of my family returned from the mountains where they were hiding. Our whole family returned to the village, but the men were still not safe—so they hid just outside the village. During this time, I was still running the family store and trying to provide for my family.

SIX

Time to Flee

ONE DAY A MAN from our village came to me at the family store and convinced me that it would be a good idea to run away from Afghanistan and go to Iran. He knew I had some money, but he did not have anything. I agreed to go with him and did not tell any of my family members. So, I got all the money from the family store one night and bought a bus ticket to Kabul. From Kabul we would find a way to Iran.

While I was at the bus station, another man who was not a Pashtun (Pashtun are mostly Talib and they are one of the tribes in Afghanistan) confronted me and said harshly, "You are a young Hazara man, and you will not be able to make it twenty miles from Mazar-E-Sharif—even to the first Taliban checkpoint. You will be forcefully removed from the bus and raped until you die."

Fear took over me; my whole body was shaking as I pondered what to do. Returning the bus ticket was my immediate reaction. I knew there was a village in the mountains in a different province, where the Taliban had been prevented from taking over because the local people were fighting against them. This was a place called Balkhab.

That evening my friend and I tried to go to Sancharak, which is a city closer to Balkhab, to try to get a bus. But, by the time we arrived there, the last truck had already left for Sancharak. We heard that we could rent a car that could catch us up quickly to the truck that had just left an hour before. Sure enough, we were able to catch this truck, and we rode on top of it all night to get to Sancharak.

Once we got to Sancharak, not knowing anyone there, we wondered how we would find our way. To the west of the city, we saw the mountainous area we had heard about and started walking in that direction. We followed the steep terrain along a river toward the top of a mountain—but without knowing if we were going in the right direction. Eventually we came across a farmer who had a couple of donkeys he let us rent to take us to the top of the mountain.

The villagers who lived in these mountainous parts had created a stair–like path that led them up and down to their village every day. As we rode these donkeys up the mountain, we came to the frightening realization that not only were we on a narrow path, but that the sheer drop of these cliffs was terrifying. It was as if the sun was swallowed up by the depths of the valley below. All I could do was close my eyes and trust these donkeys not to lose their footing and plunge us down into the pit below. When we got to the top of the mountain our relief was short-lived when we realized we had to descend back down into the actual village. Once more we had to relive the nerve–wracking experience on the mountain trail, trusting these donkeys to keep us safe.

Down in the valley below this mountain, there was a mosque that provided us shelter for the night. The villagers gave us food and welcomed us. The next day we continued on again along with our donkeys and the kind farmer who agreed to lead us to Balkhab. This three–day journey led us through beautiful mountains, clear streams, and seemingly untouched landscape. But even better than the terrain was the kindness and generosity of the local villagers, most of them Hazara. Their smiling faces and hospitality made us so proud to be Hazara—and almost made us want to stay there forever. After three days, we arrived in the beautiful village of Balkhab.

SEVEN

Crying Out to Jesus

FROM THE DAY I left our family store to when we arrived in Balkhab, it had been about three weeks. I did not know this at the time, but later I heard that my mom had suffered terribly because of my absence. After all, her thirteen–year–old son had been missing for three weeks, and not one person in my family knew where I was. My mom feared I was dead or had been kidnapped by the Taliban. She searched the prisons and some of the villages that had been overtaken by the Taliban, even looking through dead bodies to see if any among them was her son.

At this point I was done. I cried out to God: *Everything is falling apart around me and within me. I do not want to continue to live in such suffering, Lord, please take me, Relieve me. I cannot stand up under this pressure. Please release me or take me.*

Once in Balkhab, we found a hotel to stay in. The next day I met up with a few young men who were all from different cities, but all with the same purpose. Most of these young men, including myself, were desperate and hopeless.

They wanted to defend their families, their homes, and their freedoms. They longed for safety and security amidst the wars being waged all around them. For me, joining up with these men meant I would be escaping the reality of my own suffering—the bitterness and resentment, the constant reminders of what had been taken from me. But ending my life was becoming more and more of a reality. According to Shiite Muslim, if I defended myself and other innocent people against the Taliban—and got killed in the process—I would go to heaven. So, I went with those men and joined their team, not knowing how to use a gun, and not even able to carry a gun to fight the Taliban. The smallest gun was too big—bigger than me—and with crutches and walking on only one leg, it was very difficult to carry a gun like that.

At one point, I got sick there—so bad a sickness, I did not know what it was, and I could not even move. Some of my team members believed that if I would not wake up early in the morning, wash my face, and pray, I would bring a curse to our team—but if I did do those things, it would bring blessings. So, everyone was telling me to get up, wash my face, and pray.

In my heart, I was praying to all the prophets I knew of and using all the religions I had studied to bring about my healing—but I felt that nobody heard me. I went toward a stream to wash my face—and possibly my whole body—in the water, hobbling along with the crutches. From our room to the stream was about a mile; then I had to descend three or four feet and walk a little farther to the water. So, as I was walking down, drained of all my energy, something happened—and I fell with the crutches and hit my head on a big rock.

I could not move. It was hard, I wanted to cry—but I

could not. I wanted to yell or shout, but I could not do anything because I was so weak. Inside of me I felt a huge darkness. I felt like I was going to die and that I was breathing my last. As I cried inside with pain, I called out, "Jesus, I am crying, I am praying to you, I know you are one of the important prophets—please heal me." I prayed and cried to Jesus for a while.

After I prayed, I got up and walked toward the water to wash my face and to clean up. That night I slept well. The next morning when I woke up, I felt normal—no sickness, no problems—I just had forgotten what happened to me. Other people asked me if I was feeling well, and I responded, "Yeah, what happened?"

They replied, "You were sick."

Then the memory came back, and I realized I had been sick for a few days, but now I was healthy—like nothing ever happened. From that point on, there was something in my heart that wanted to know more about Christ.

EIGHT

Questions for God

WE MOVED to another big valley where there were more people and more fighting. I kept thinking my life would end in some fight there. It was full of armed conflict between the Taliban and the local people. The Taliban fight during the daytime, and the people fight at night. I wanted to join the night fights, but I had no experience and no ability to fight well. Because I wanted to die anyway, I had no fear. I tried and went into battle, but it was a scary situation—and too hard to walk in the dark with crutches in the mountains.

That valley had been so beautiful—surrounded by mountains and full of trees. Then the Taliban took over and burned everything in the valley. In a tiny village they destroyed everything—shops, houses, trees, and farms. I got so mad at them and asked God, *Why would you allow so much suffering? Why, God, does the evil Taliban do bad things and you do not care? Why, God, did I lose a leg? Why is the Taliban killing us because of being Hazar? Did you make us Hazara just to live and killed?*

I had a million questions for God. I questioned his mercy and his ability. So many mountains and beautiful places where I used to hike, and I thought I could save people from the top of these mountains if I stayed there when the Taliban came. I wanted to fight from the top of those mountains and save lives as a young man. I was thinking and planning to die and be a hero!

NINE

I Want to be Like Samson

I TRIED to find things I could sell to make some money because the Taliban destroyed everything. We did not have enough food. We survived by the vegetable which grew on the ground freely or fruit we found hanging on the trees. After a few weeks digging in the burned stores and houses, I pulled out a lot of aluminum and copper and sold it. I did not eat, but I bought a radio with the money that I got from the scrap metal. The radio did not work inside the village, so every morning when I woke up, I would go to the top of the mountain and listen to the radio. I could not find many stations, but one of them was a Christian station telling stories from the Old Testament.

I listened every day, and one day they were talking about Samson. For some reason I was so emotional that day that, after hearing the story of Samson, something deep down in my heart said, "Wow, I just want to be a Samson." Up until then, I had been doing all this crazy stuff to try and save *one* person, but at that moment I got the idea that

I should save a *lot* of people and then die—just like Samson.

After hearing this story, I fantasized a lot by walking around the mountain and strategizing where I should position myself during a fight. I had to be ready to run to this mountain or that mountain to save people and kill all the Taliban. I could not really do that, of course, but it was a dream. For the next couple of months, war would come and go. Either it would stop before it got to us, or the Taliban would not even come. I had been in a small battle many times, but nothing significant ever happened. *Oh, my gosh, what's going on?* I wondered. *I want to die and save somebody's life and go to heaven!*

TEN

Looking for Christians

IN 2001, American troops went into Afghanistan and killed the Taliban. So, I went home and reunited with my mom. She was very glad to see me. So, I started working as an electrician and made a lot of money. I was quite happy doing that, but still there was something inside my heart that kept asking, "Now what?" This life had no meaning, and I thought I had to do something else. I decided to earn a lot of money so I could be "a good human being."

I did any kind of job to earn money. It allowed my dad to stop working at his store. I sent my brothers to trade school to finish their education. At fifteen or sixteen years of age I worked by myself, often putting in twelve hours a day. I would make transformers, do wiring, whatever I could— all to earn more money to give to my family. I just wanted to sacrifice my life and do something good for them.

I started getting into another business, buying electronic equipment then sending to a different province. I made mistakes and lost most of the money. I thought, *What now? All my money is gone. Now I'm going to be a beggar!* My brother had always said I was going to be a beggar because I had only one leg, and people would find it easier to give because of that. I hated it, and I did not want to be that person.

Something in my heart was pushing me to seek out Christ. In Mazar I told some of my three friends that I wanted to be a Christian. They said they wanted the same thing! So, four of us decided we wanted to become Christians, and they put me in charge. "You have to lead us and direct us to this," they said.

I went to Herat and Kabul, looking for Christians—but found none. I even asked some Afghan guards who were working for foreign offices if they knew Christians. "I want to know about Christianity," I insisted—but they thought I was joking and told me to get out. They brushed me off as young and immature.

I told them, "No, I'm serious, I want to talk to some Christians."

I started talking bad and fighting them. I had lots of anger and frustration. My heart was restless and full of worries, always seeking something and not reaching it, always wanting something more—but I did not know what it was. I found no one in Kabul, so I went back to Mazar and told my friends. "I found no Christians—none. No Christians anywhere, I guess."

"Did you find a Bible?" they asked.

"No, I did not." So, I told them, "I'm going to leave Afghanistan and go to Iran and from there maybe to Greece or Ireland."

I asked them if they want to come, and they said no. I did not have a passport or enough money to buy a passport. One of them did have a passport, so I took off his picture and put mine and tried to go to Iran. But I could not get into the country with that because they knew it was not mine. So, I found a smuggler who paid the police, and they took my passport and let me in. That's how I got into Iran. Then I found another three friends staying in Iran who had grown up with me and had run away from the Taliban. I met them in Mashhad and told them I was going to Turkey and then to Greece.

They said, "Okay, we want to do that, too!"

So, we all packed and said, "Let's go."

ELEVEN

The Rough Road to Turkey

SOME OF US HAD MONEY, but I did not. I was thinking how I could manipulate the smuggler and run away from them in Turkey. Two of us did get to Turkey, but then one went to England after three months. One went to Ireland, and I stayed in Iran until I could save money working there.

In May of 2007 I talked with a man who was a trafficker/smuggler. Because we did not have any passports, we had to go through the mountains (which had a lot of snow at that time). He said we were going to take a car or ride a horse to pass the border, but after that we were going to walk. I told him, "Hey, I have only one leg, I need to ride a car or a horse or something." (The current leg I have is very good, but the one I had at that time was terrible.) My makeshift leg was a mess, cobbled together with plastic and ropes and tape. When I walked, people would hear from 100 meters away Ali's lag noise.

He said, "Yeah, do not worry. When we get to the border, we will not walk."

There were eighteen of us, and they brought three horses. To me they gave a big, crazy horse with no saddle or anything. Another guy rode with me on back, but he did not know anything about horses, either—not even how to sit on a horse. This mountain pass was very dangerous. If you fell off the path, you would not survive. I was so afraid. *I have gone through all these crazy things,* I thought, *and this is how I am going to die?*

It was a very hard road. I finally told the smuggler, "I need to either walk or get this other guy off the horse," but he told me it was not his problem.

So, I started walking until I got tired, then I would ride the horse a little, switching on and off with other people. All night we walked and rode the horses. It was snowing heavily—we would have been lost if not for our guide. We stayed at a place to rest so we could travel the next night into the city. For three days we stayed in a house, and he the smuggler kept bringing more and more people in. There were over forty of us in a small room with nothing to do, and we could not really sleep because we could not lie down.

I started building friendships with some of the other people. I told them, "I will tell you a story, sing you a song, whatever you want me to do!" so that they would help me get over the mountain when it was too hard for my bad leg. I asked them if they would carry my pack or carry me or push me—whatever was needed. They agreed, so for three days I was singing and telling stories—mostly the Samson story—or some of the experiences and difficulty I lived during the Taliban.

TWELVE

Barely Made It

FINALLY, the guide came back with a car and took us about an hour up the mountain. We had to walk part of the way because of some police in the streets. He picked us back up in his car, but his tires blew out a short time later—so we had to walk again anyway. It was going to take us all night to cross the mountain. We started at 9:30 p.m., and it would take to the end of the night to finish the trek. It was very difficult crossing the snow, and I could not do it. Many people had helped push me, pull me, carry my stuff, but I got to the point where I was exhausted and had to lie down. I was done. I was not going to go on any longer. Everyone left except for two or three guys. As I lay in the snow, I told them, "Do not worry about me. Just leave me, and I will die here. You keep going."

They were crying and saying, "We are not going to leave you here! We will not go without you—if you do not go, we will not go!"

They kept encouraging me, and finally I pushed myself up. One guy got my backpack and two other guys helped me walk. We had to hike several more hours before we got to the city, but we finally made it.

When we got to Van—the city in Turkey—I stayed with the trafficker for twenty days until I was kicked out. He did not know how to get me to Istanbul by car, and I was not going to walk again—so he just kicked me out of the car and onto the street. I did not know the language, I did not know the city, I did not know anything. I walked around the city hoping to find someone who would let me stay with them. Eventually I introduced myself to the United Nations and asked them for help. They gave me a hotel room and a card that would allow me to stay in the city.

THIRTEEN

Finally, a Church!

THE FIRST NIGHT in the hotel, an Iranian guy came up to me. We talked and became friends. He started complaining that there was a church nearby where people were converting to Christianity—an Afghan family, a lot of Iranians, and many others.

When I heard that, my heart exploded and I began to run around saying, "You have to take me to that church! Take me right now!"

I was crying and yelling, begging him to take me. He thought I was crazy.

"What's going on?" he asked. "Why do you want to go to the church? Are you Christian or Muslim?"

I said that I did not know what was going on, but I knew I needed to go to the church. Yes, I had been raised a Muslim—but I wanted to go to the church. It was closed, but he promised to take me when it opened.

I started going to the church as often as I could. I went every Sunday and began to build relationships with people at the church. Whenever I would go, I felt joy and love and peace in my heart. I had never felt any of those things before in my life. I had had a very hard life, growing up in the mountains during heavy fighting. But in the church, there was peace—a real God was there. For several months I continued to go to church and to their Bible studies. But when I would leave the church, something would be missing. I would start worrying, start arguing with people, and just get into a lot of stupid trouble.

During this time, I made friends with many Muslims, but especially a very nice Afghan family who invited me to their house a lot for lunch and for dinner. The father knew I was Muslim but was going to the church all the time. I had not been to a mosque since I started going to the church. He warned me not to go to church.

"Why?" I asked.

"You will become a Christian."

"Yes, I probably will! I love it and I really like the church. There are a lot of good things inside the church."

He told me, "No, the Christians are crazy and nonsense. They believe that Christ is the Son of God and that he suffered and he's this and that. It does not make sense!"

"Yes, I know it does not make sense, but I like it!"

"You will lose your family, your parents, your friends."

We had just been eating the food they provided. I was a refugee in a foreign land—a young, single guy who did not know how to cook and did not have family. "I do not care!" I retorted.

"If you become a Christian, you will lose my friendship."

Oh, my gosh! I thought, *I do not want to lose the food!*

After such a long time, having found this family, they

are going to treat me like this? I said I was going to keep going to the church. So, that was the end of our friendship. They no longer invited me to their house, and we did not talk much anymore.

FOURTEEN

A New Life—With Struggles

EVENTUALLY, I became a Christian and got baptized after six or seven months of attending the church. The church was always telling me, "Christ is changing you. Christ is giving you a new identity. Christ is giving you the Holy Spirit."

"Okay, yes! I want it all. I want the peace, the life, the joy, I want to have a good life and not be who I was in my previous life." But even after I became a Christian, I was still the same, behaving very badly.

I leased a big apartment and started renting out part of it to other people. I did this so I could make enough money to live there. But I charged the other tenants a little extra.

One day, one of them approached me and said, "This is not right. You're taking too much money." Then five of them came, and we got into an argument. I was being stubborn and wanted my money.

"You are renting from me!" I insisted.

"No, we will split this fairly," they countered.

We then got into a fight, and they beat me badly. My

face was very bruised, I got a broken nose, could not really
see, and had a hard time hearing. I called my pastor and
told him, "I got into a fight, and they beat me very badly. I
do not really care about that, though. What I want to know
is, why isn't Christ changing me? Why am I still the same
person?"

He told me to come to the church and we prayed. After
a few weeks, as I prayed more and learned more, God
started changing me. Looking back on where I was, I see He
transformed me so much! I no longer felt the way I did
before. I really felt like I was living in heaven. Christ
became my joy, and every day I would wake up with peace
and would feel His grace. Every day I was telling people
about Christ. And I started to notice that God began doing
amazing things among the Afghan people. Many became
believers and many of their lives were changed. All of this
happened while I was there in Turkey, and all happened
through my witness and testimony.

FIFTEEN

A Great Transformation

EVENTUALLY, the United Nations gave me a visa and the status of refugee. I came to America—to Phoenix, Arizona —on November 5, 2009. At first in Phoenix, it was very rough. I spoke no English, had no friends or family, no contacts—and only $50. Two weeks after I arrived, they started pressuring me to work, but I did not know what to do, where to work, or what I could do with my leg and my lack of understanding English. I felt the stress of living in America, even as a follower of Christ. It seemed like home-less people were under bridges and everywhere—and I thought it could happen to me. After all, hardly anyone knew me, and no one seemed to care.

My name is Mohammad Ali and, yes, I'm from Afghanistan. It's nothing short of a miracle—many mira-cles, actually—what God did in my life. Here I was, someone who had survived war, the loss of a leg, and living as a refugee in America—all while still a fairly young man. God was working in my personal life, guiding me and saving me from physical and spiritual death. The more I had wanted to die, the more God wanted to save me. He rescued me from myself—from dark thoughts and harrowing situations—all for His glory. He gave me a new desire to live for Christ. Thanks be to Him for what He has enabled me to overcome—I am totally amazed by it!

SIXTEEN

A Bridge to Others

GOD HAS PUT me in an unusual situation—an Afghan Christian with a Muslim background. I know both Islam and Christianity, spiritually and historically. Despite their vastly different worldviews, I can relate to people from both sides, because I have lived in both. When I'm among Muslims, they're reasonably comfortable with me because I am from Afghanistan, but they do question how I could be a follower of Christ (they think it's impossible). When I am with Christians, they wonder how I can love Muslims when I have converted from Islam to Christianity. But I believe part of my calling is to be a peacemaker and bridge-builder between the two faiths. When I build friendships with Muslim friends and help them with physical needs, it helps them to see God. It gives me a platform to share the truth of the gospel. My own journey has seen so many ups and downs that I can relate to almost anyone.

After more than a decade in the US, I stay involved in relationships with international friends, both Christian and non-Christian. I am intentional about meeting people locally, and I make a point of being engaged in their lives. Especially with non-Christians, my personal history and my love for them attract them to God. I organize and participate in hiking trips, soccer games, community picnics, and dinners in my home to help foster relationships with people in the local community.

I have been invited to speak in a number of different churches. When people hear that I am from Afghanistan, they ask a lot of questions. This gives me an opportunity to highlight the differences between Islam and Christianity and to inform them of the suffering that exists in other parts of the world, especially in Afghanistan. I know it well because I lived there and suffered myself. Most Americans have no idea how Christians or God-seekers struggle in other parts of the world.

SEVENTEEN

Ministry in America

HOW ELSE HAVE I invested my life since coming to America? Besides working various jobs to support myself, my ministry heart has been directed toward assisting other refugees in a variety of ways. I have helped more than thirty of them enroll in different schools and more than fifty of them (women and men) get jobs. I have worked part-time at a church, helping to build bridges between Muslims and Christians. And after finishing two years of school and improving my English language skills, I worked for a while as a cultural advisor and translator. My improved ability to converse—and my commitment to the faith—encouraged me to invite many Muslim friends to church.

All the while, I have regularly hosted get-togethers in my home where Muslims and Christians could eat together and learn to understand each other better. My ministry is to facilitate connecting people from different nations and different faiths, helping them understand each other and share their life histories and experiences together. This helps to develop a deeper understanding and respect for each other. As we get to know a culture, then a people group, and then a nation, we come to expand our horizons about the rest of the world—and it thereby helps us to serve our God better.

After eight years in Phoenix, Arizona, I decided to relocate to Colorado Springs, Colorado. But before I actually moved on October 1, 2017, I was invited to speak to a small study group at a church in Phoenix about how Christians could minister to refugees. Two weeks later they asked me to come back and speak to the whole church. In the course of those engagements, I met a lovely Christian woman at the church who has since become my wife. After our wedding in January 2018, we settled in Colorado Springs. The Lord has since blessed us with a beautiful baby girl, born in November 2020.

Together with my wife, we continue to minister to refugees in America. I am a refugee myself, so I feel the pain and fears that many refugees experience. I know the culture, the language, and the characteristics of both the Christian and Islamic communities. I sense that my calling is to care for refugees and Muslims who have suffered just as I have. But I am also ministering through social media and telephone to the growing church inside Afghanistan, serving as a mentor, discipler, and advisor. My life has been so dramatically transformed by the love and power of Jesus Christ that I want to share that new life with others. I want to light the love of Christ in their lives and bring the hope of Christ to their families!

CPSIA information can be obtained
at www.ICGtesting.com
Printed in the USA
BVHW081921280623
666441BV00005B/1168

9 781955 043595